Beats Me, Claude

Story by Joan Lowery Nixon

Pictures by Tracey Campbell Pearson

Puffin Books

PUFFIN BOOKS
Published by the Penguin Group
Viking Penguin Inc., 40 West 23rd Street, New York, New York 10010, U.S.A.
Penguin Books Ltd, 27 Wrights Lane, London W8 5TZ, England
Penguin Books Australia Ltd, Ringwood, Victoria, Australia
Penguin Books Canada Ltd, 2801 John Street, Markham, Ontario, Canada L3R 1B4
Penguin Books (N.Z.) Ltd, 182–190 Wairau Road, Auckland 10, New Zealand

Penguin Books Ltd, Registered Offices: Harmondsworth, Middlesex, England

First published in the United States of America by Viking Penguin Inc., 1986
Published in Picture Puffins 1988
1   3   5   7   9   10   8   6   4   2
Text copyright © Joan Lowery Nixon, 1986
Illustrations copyright © Tracey Campbell Pearson, 1986
All rights reserved   Library of Congress catalog number: 88-42871
ISBN 0-14-050847-3
Printed in the United States of America by Lake Book Manufacturers, Melrose Park, Illinois
Set in Cheltenham Book

For Clay —
We hope you have better
luck making an apple pie
than Shirley did! We hope
you like this as much as
we do!
Love,
Peter & Eliza

CHAPTER ONE

Shirley and Claude stood in the doorway of their cabin in that great state called Texas. The hills below them rolled like soft green waves into the distance, and the morning sky was puffed with cotton-white clouds.

"Shirley," Claude said, "this sure does seem to be the peaceful place we was lookin' for."

Shirley gave a sigh. "Maybe too peaceful," she said. "Sometimes I hanker for someone else to talk to. Why, sometimes my mouth gets so set on talkin' to someone that I talk to that ugly old moose head hangin' on the wall."

"You're not the only one whose mouth's set for somethin'," Claude said. "Lately my mouth's been set for an apple pie like my mama used to make, all bubbly and spicy and oozin' out of the crust."

"That so?" Shirley said. "Then I reckon I'll make you an apple pie for your noon meal, Claude."

So while Claude was out in the fields, Shirley tied on her apron and pulled a sack of apples out of the root cellar.

Shirley never was a very good cook, so she chunked some lard into a bowl, poured in some water, and dumped in enough flour to make it stick together. She slammed it on the table and stuffed half in the bottom of her iron skillet. She put in some sliced apples, then covered them with the other half of the dough. She put a lid on the whole thing and set it in the fireplace. "Seems I'm forgettin' somethin'," Shirley said. "But I can't think of what."

She had no sooner cleaned up the kitchen than she heard a knock at the door. She opened it to find a sour-faced man, wearing a black suit, who was gripping the shoulder of a boy about ten years of age.

"I'm a preacher," the man said, "and I'm trying to find the road to Austin, where I can take this poor, unfortunate orphan to be cared for."

"I'll show you," Shirley said, "but have something to eat first."

As soon as the man had left to wash up, the boy said, "I'm Tom. I'm a real orphan, but he's not a real preacher. He left my sister with a woman in town. She paid him twenty dollars so my sister could stay there and scrub the floor and wash pots. And he's going to sell me, too."

The man came back and sat at the table, under the moose head. "You said you had something to eat?"

The lid of the iron skillet was rising and wobbling. Shirley guessed the pie must be about done. She put the skillet on the table, in front of the man. He leaned forward to take off the lid.

"Hold it," Shirley said. She picked up her rifle. "A real preacher would 'turn a few words of thanks afore startin' to eat. Be on your way. Tom stays here."

The man angrily slammed his fists on the table.

With a loud swoosh the pie exploded, splattering apples and dough all over him. He yelled something awful.

"Dang!" Shirley said. "Now I recollect. I was supposed to cut slits in the crust so the steam could get out." Being tenderhearted, she dumped a bucket of water over the man to cool him down.

He jumped up so fast one foot stuck tight in the bucket. He scrambled out of the door, climbed on his horse, and galloped past Claude, who had just stepped into the clearing.

Claude thought on it a moment. "Any reason why that feller's ridin' around yellin' with his foot in a bucket?"

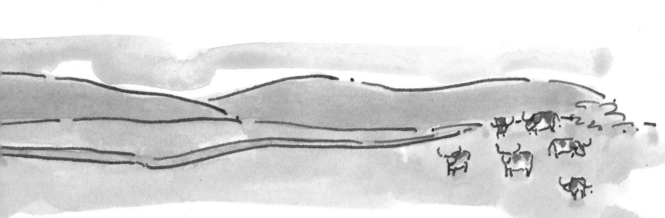

"He got a mite upset when my apple pie blew up," Shirley said.

"Any reason why you can't make a regular bubbly, spicy, oozy apple pie like other folks?" Claude asked.

Shirley shrugged. "Beats me, Claude," she said.

CHAPTER TWO

Shirley explained about Tom while they ate their noon meal, but Claude said, "No way to have peace and quiet with a ten-year-old boy in the house. You can take him back to town tomorrow, Shirley."

As he strode to the door, Claude added, "I'm really hankerin' for an apple pie, Shirley. I hope you're fixin' to try your hand at another one."

Shirley never was a very good cook, so she chunked some lard into a bowl, poured in some water, and dumped in enough flour to make it stick together. She slammed it all on the table and stuffed half into the iron skillet. She put in some sliced apples, then covered them with the other half of the dough. This time she cut slits in the crust before she put on the lid and set the skillet in the fireplace. "Seems like I'm forgettin' somethin' again," Shirley said, "but I can't think of what."

Meanwhile Tom had cleaned up the kitchen and was sweeping the floor.

"I'm mighty beholden to you, Tom," she said.

"I always done chores at home," Tom said. "Afore Mama got sick, she even learned us to cook."

Well, Shirley got out some sweet milk and sorry-looking ginger cookies and sat down to hear Tom's story.

He had just finished the telling, and Shirley was wiping away a tear, when the door burst open and a man with a black kerchief around his neck stomped in. He waved a gun at Shirley and Tom, dropped a bank sack on the table, and sat down under the moose head.

"This seems as good a place as any to hole up while the sheriff's lookin' for me," he said. "What's in the skillet?"

"Apple pie," Shirley said.

"Bring it over here," the bank robber said.

So Shirley put the skillet on the table in front of him. Very carefully she took off the lid.

"Don't smell too good," he said, "but apple pie's apple pie." He dug into it with his fork and stuffed a piece into his mouth.

Then he jumped to his feet, yelling, "That's no apple pie!" And he shot his gun at the skillet.

The bullet bounced off the bottom crust and got the old moose head right between the eyes. The moose head dropped straight down on the head of the bank robber and stuck tight.

"Dang!" Shirley said. "Now I recollect. I was supposed to put sweet'nin' in the pie." She grabbed the man's gun and shoved him into the chair. Then she fired a shot out the window, hoping to attract attention.

It wasn't long before the sheriff poked his head in the door. "Got your man," Shirley said.

"Good for you, Shirley," the sheriff said. "There's a fifty-dollar reward on this fellow. Next time you're in town you can collect."

"I'll be there," Shirley said. "By the way, you can keep that moose head on him till you get to town. I don't want it back."

The sheriff and the robber rode past Claude as he stepped into the clearing. Claude thought on it for a moment, then came into the cabin. "Any reason why the sheriff's arrestin' a moose?"

"He shot my apple pie," Shirley said.

Claude put a finger into the pie and tasted it. "Think he done it a favor," he said. "Any reason why you can't make a regular, bubbly, spicy, oozy apple pie like other folks?"

Shirley shrugged. "Beats me, Claude," she said.

CHAPTER THREE

"Claude," Shirley said before Claude headed back outside, "let's talk about keepin' Tom."

"Nope," Claude said. "It's noisy enough around here. Back he goes to town tomorrow." He walked to the door. "Shirley, you just don't know how I've been hankerin' for apple pie. Think you could get another one baked afore supper?"

"I reckon so," Shirley said.

Now Shirley never was a very good cook, so she chunked some lard into a bowl, poured in some water, and dumped in enough flour to make it stick together. She slammed it on the table and stuffed half into her skillet. This time she threw in a couple of handfuls of sugar, poured in a slurp of honey and a lot of molasses. She covered it with dough, cut slits in the crust, put a lid on the skillet, and set it in the fireplace. "Seems like I'm forgettin' somethin' again," Shirley said, "but I can't think of what."

Tom said, "Meanin' no disrespect, but you don't make apple pie the way my mama learned me, all bubbly, spicy, and oozy."

Shirley's pie began bubbling and oozing all over the fireplace.

"Maybe I could make another," Tom said, polite-like. "Just in case." And he set to work fashioning a little oven out of a piece of tin and some bricks.

Just as Tom put his pie into the oven, Shirley heard horses. Moments later the door nearly slammed off its hinges. Three men in ragged uniforms raced in.

"Don't move!" the first man yelled.

The second swept off his tattered army hat and bowed. "We'll soon be on our way, ma'am. We just need to stay under cover for a while."

"I think they're running away from the U.S. Army!" Tom whispered to Shirley.

The third man had his eyes on the skillet. "What's in that pan?" he asked.

"Apple pie," Shirley said.

"I'd sure like some of that pie," he said. The three men sat down.

Shirley carried the skillet and three forks to the table. She edged slowly toward her rifle.

The men waved dripping chunks of pie in the air to cool them, then stuck them into their mouths.

The first man grabbed his throat. The second man bent over double, and the third man shouted, "We've been poisoned!"

"Dang!" Shirley said. "Now I recollect. I was supposed to put in the apples." She pointed her rifle at them. "Hold it right there," she said. "Any man who moves is gonna find himself eatin' that whole pie."

None of them moved. Tom took their guns while Shirley fired out the window, hoping to attract attention.

It didn't take long for a U.S. Army patrol to arrive. And in only a few moments the prisoners were being led away to the sound of the army bugle.

The patrol leader saluted Claude as they passed him at the edge of the clearing.

Claude thought on it a moment. Then he came into the cabin. "Shirley, any reason why the U.S. Army's parading through our property?"

"They was after some prisoners who got done in by my apple pie," Shirley said.

Claude put a finger into the pie, then put it in his mouth. He made a terrible face.

Before he could complain, Shirley said, "Just smell the apple pie Tom is makin'!"

From Tom's oven were coming all the bubbly, spicy, oozy, cinnamon-sugar smells an apple pie ought to have.

Claude watched Tom take the pie from the oven and place it, all golden and buttery, on the table. Shirley cut a great slab of pie and laid it in front of Claude.

He raised a bite on his fork, then slowly put it into his mouth. As he chewed he smiled and tears came to his eyes. "It's even better than my mama's pie," he said.

"If Tom lived here he could make you an apple pie like that every time you hankered for one," Shirley said.

Claude beamed at Tom. "Set down, son. Let's talk about the two of us buildin' on an extra room at the side of the house."

"Claude," Shirley said. "Tom and I need to go into town tomorrow and pick up some things he left behind."

"What things?" Claude asked.

Shirley cut Claude another piece of pie. "Just some clothes, some books, and a sister."

"Fine by me," Claude said, his mind on the pie. "Shirley, is there any reason why you could never learn to make a pie like this?"

Shirley's smile was so bright it lit up half the cabin. "Beats me, Claude!" she said.